# The Quiltmaker's Gift

Story by
**Jeff Brumbeau**

Pictures by
**Gail de Marcken**

SCHOLASTIC INC.
New York  Toronto  London  Auckland  Sydney
Mexico City  New Delhi  Hong Kong  Buenos Aires

ISBN     0-439-29143-7

Text copyright © 2000 by Jeff Brumbeau.
Watercolors copyright © 2000 by Gail de Marcken. All rights reserved.
Published by Scholastic Inc. SCHOLASTIC and associated logos
are trademarks and/or registered
trademarks of Scholastic Inc.

12 11 10 9 8 7 6 5 4 3 2 1                    2 3 4 5 6 7/0

                                                    09

Printed in the U.S.A.

First Scholastic paperback printing, October 2002
Editorial Director: Nancy Loving Tubesing
Art Director: Joy Morgan Dey

*For Marcia, who with the gift of herself has given me everything.*

*—Jeff*


*To B with love.*

*—Gail*

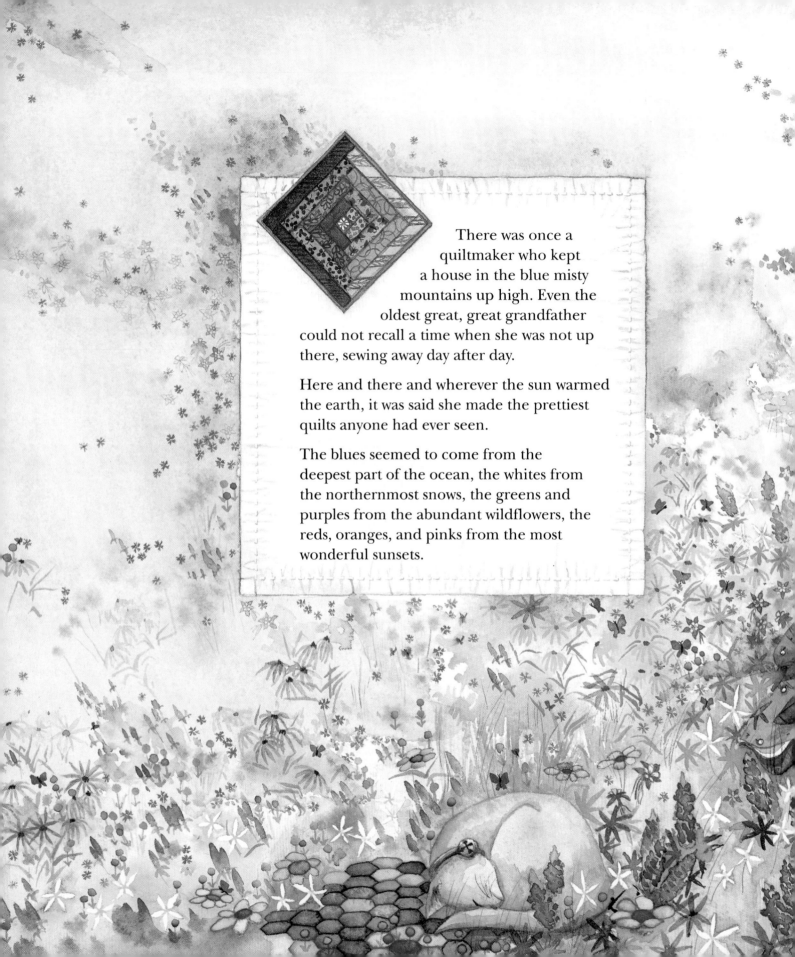

There was once a quiltmaker who kept a house in the blue misty mountains up high. Even the oldest great, great grandfather could not recall a time when she was not up there, sewing away day after day.

Here and there and wherever the sun warmed the earth, it was said she made the prettiest quilts anyone had ever seen.

The blues seemed to come from the deepest part of the ocean, the whites from the northernmost snows, the greens and purples from the abundant wildflowers, the reds, oranges, and pinks from the most wonderful sunsets.

Some said there was magic in her fingers. Some whispered that her needles and cloth were gifts of the bewitched. And still others said the quilts really fell to earth from the shoulders of passing angels.

Many people climbed her mountain, pockets bursting with gold, hoping to buy one of the wonderful quilts. But the woman would not sell them.

"I give my quilts to those who are poor or homeless," she told all who knocked on her door. "They are not for the rich."

On the darkest and coldest nights, the woman would make her way down the mountain to the town below. There she would wander the cobblestone streets until she came upon someone sleeping outside in the chill. She would then take a newly finished quilt from her bag, wrap it around their shivering shoulders, tuck them in tight, and tiptoe away.

Then the very next morning, with a steaming cup of blackberry tea, she would begin a new quilt.

Now at this time
there also lived a very
powerful and greedy king
who liked nothing better than
to receive presents.

The hundreds of thousands of beautiful gifts
he got for Christmas and his birthday were
never enough. So a law was passed that the
king would celebrate his birthday twice a year.

When that still wasn't enough, he ordered his
soldiers to search the kingdom for those few
people who had not yet given him a gift.

Over the years, the king had come to own
almost all of the prettiest things in the world.
Throughout the castle, from top to bottom,
in drawers and on shelves, in boxes and
trunks and closets and sacks, all of the
king's countless things were stashed.

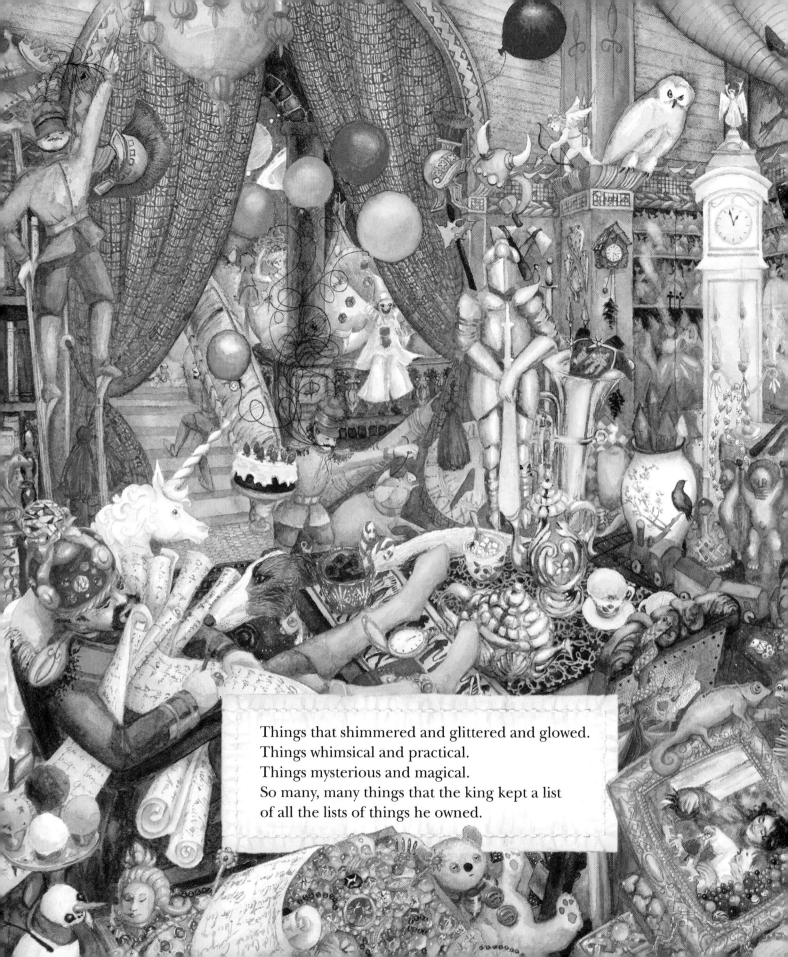

Things that shimmered and glittered and glowed.
Things whimsical and practical.
Things mysterious and magical.
So many, many things that the king kept a list
of all the lists of things he owned.

And yet with all these
marvelous treasures to
enjoy, the king never smiled.
He was not happy at all.
"Somewhere there must be one beautiful thing
that will finally make me happy," he was often
heard to say. "And I will have it!"

One day a soldier rushed into the palace with
news about a magical quiltmaker who lived in
the mountains. The king stamped his foot.
"And how is it that this person has never given
me one of her quilts as a gift?" he demanded.

"She only makes them for the poor, Your
Majesty," the soldier replied. "And she will not
sell them for any amount of money."

"Well, we shall see about that!" the king roared.
"Bring me a horse and a thousand soldiers."
And they set off in search of the quiltmaker.

But when they arrived at her house, the
quiltmaker merely laughed. "My quilts are for
the poor and needy, and I can easily see that
you are neither."

"I want one of those quilts!" the king
demanded. "It might be the one thing that will
finally make me happy."

The woman thought
for a moment.

"Make presents of everything
you own," she said, "and then
I'll make a quilt for you. With each gift that
you give, I'll sew in another piece. When at
last all your things are gone, your quilt will
be finished."

"Give away all my wonderful treasures?" cried
the king. "I don't give things away, I take them."
And with that he ordered his soldiers to seize
the beautiful star quilt from the quiltmaker.

But when they rushed upon her, she tossed
the quilt out the window, and a great gust
of wind carried it up, up and away.

The king was now very angry. He marched the woman down through town and up another mountain where he had his royal iron-makers shape a thick bracelet of iron. Then they chained her to a rock in the cave of a sleeping bear.

Once more the king asked her for a quilt, and once more she refused.

"Very well then," the king replied. "I'll leave you here. And when the bear awakens, I'm sure he will make a very fine breakfast of you."

Later, when the bear's eyes opened and he saw the woman in his cave, he stood on his mighty hind legs and gave a roar that rattled her bones. She looked up at him and sadly shook her head.

"It's no wonder you're so grouchy," the quiltmaker said. "You've nothing but rocks on which to rest your head at night. Bring me an armful of pine needles and with my shawl, I'll make you a great big pillow."

And that is what she did. No one had ever been so kind to the bear before. So he broke the iron bracelet and asked her to spend the night.

Now although the king was very good at being greedy, he was very bad at being mean. All that night he could not sleep for thinking about the poor woman in the cave.

"Oh my, oh my, what have I done?" he wailed.

So he woke up his soldiers and they all marched in their pajamas up to the cave to save her. But when they arrived, the king found the quiltmaker and the bear having a breakfast of berries and honey.

Now the king completely forgot about feeling sorry and became angry all over again. He ordered the royal island-makers to build an island barely big enough for the woman to stand on her tiptoes.

Once again the king asked her for a quilt, and once again she said no.

"Very well," the king replied. "Tonight when you're too tired to stand, and lie down to sleep, you'll drown." And the king left her alone on the tiny island.

Shortly after he left, the quiltmaker saw a sparrow flying across the great lake. A cold, fierce wind was blowing and it did not look like the poor bird would make it to shore. The quiltmaker called to him and he stopped to rest on her shoulder. The poor, tired sparrow was shivering, so the woman quickly made him a coat from scraps of her purple vest.

When he was warmed and the wind had stopped, the bird flew off. But he was very grateful to the quiltmaker for what she had done.

Soon the sky darkened as the air filled with a huge cloud of sparrows. Thousands of wings beating together, they swooped down, lifted the woman in their little beaks, and carried her safely to shore.

Again that night, the king could not sleep for thinking about the woman alone on the island.

"Oh my, oh my, what have I done?" he moaned.

So he woke up his sleepy soldiers again and they marched in their pajamas down to the lake to set the woman free. But when they arrived, she was sitting on a tree limb sewing tiny purple coats for all the sparrows.

"I give up!" the king shouted. "What must I do for you to give me a quilt?"

"As I said," the woman answered, "give away all of the things you own and I'll sew a quilt for you. And with each gift that you give, I'll add another piece to your quilt."

"I can't do that!" cried the king. "I love all my wonderful, beautiful things."

"But if they don't make you happy," the woman replied, "what good are they?"

"That's true," the king sighed. And he thought about what she had said for a long, long time. So long that weeks went by.

"Oh, all right," he finally muttered, "if I must give away my treasures, then I must!"

The king went to his
castle and searched from
top to bottom for something
he could bear to give away.

Frowning, he finally came out
with a single marble. But the boy who received it
smiled so brightly in return, the king went back for
more things.

Eventually, he brought out a pile of velvet coats
and went about the town, giving them to people
dressed only in rags. All were so pleased that they
marched up and down the street in a grand parade.

Still, the king did not smile.

Next the king fetched a hundred waltzing blue Siamese cats and the dozen fish that were clear as glass.

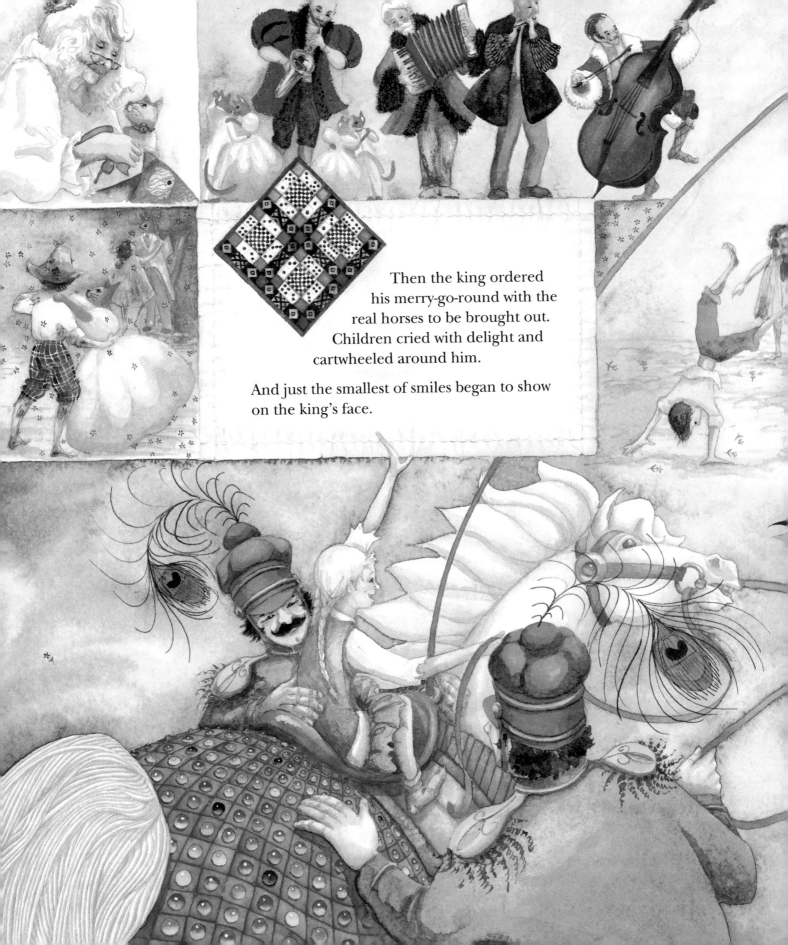

Then the king ordered
his merry-go-round with the
real horses to be brought out.
Children cried with delight and
cartwheeled around him.

And just the smallest of smiles began to show
on the king's face.

The king looked about him and saw the dancing and merrymaking and all the happiness his gifts had brought. A child took hold of his hand and pulled him into the dance. Now the king really smiled and even laughed out loud.

"How can this be?" he cried. "How can I feel so happy about giving my things away? Bring everything out! Bring it all out at once!"

Meanwhile, the quiltmaker kept her word and started making a special quilt for the king. With each gift that he gave, she added another piece to his quilt.

So the king kept on giving and giving.

When at last there was no one left in town who had not received something, the king decided to go out into the world and find others who might be in need of his gifts.

But before he left, the king promised the quiltmaker he would send a sparrow back to her each and every time he gave something away.

Morning, noon, and night, the wagons rolled out of town, each piled high with the king's wonderful things. And for years and years, messenger sparrows flew to the quiltmaker's windowsill as the king slowly emptied his wagons, trading his treasures for smiles around the world.

On and on the quiltmaker worked, and piece by piece the king's quilt grew more and more beautiful.

Finally, one day a weary sparrow flew into her window and perched on her needle.

She knew then and there that it was the last messenger, so she put a final stitch in the quilt and started down the mountain in search of the king.

After a long search,
she finally found him.
The king's royal clothes
were now in tatters and his toes
poked out of his boots. Yet his
eyes glittered with joy and his laugh was
wonderful and thunderous.

The quiltmaker unfolded the king's quilt
from her bag. It was so beautiful that
hummingbirds and butterflies fluttered
about. Standing on tiptoe, she tenderly
wrapped it around him.

"What's this?" cried the king.

"As I promised you long ago," the woman
said, "when the day came that you, yourself,
were poor, only then would I give you a
quilt." The king's great sunny laugh made
green apples fall and flowers turn his way.

"But I am not poor," he said. "I may look
poor, but in truth my heart is full to
bursting, filled with memories of all the
happiness I've given and received. I'm the
richest man I know."

"Nevertheless," the quiltmaker said, "I made
this quilt just for you."

"Thank you," replied the king. "I'll take it, but only if you'll accept a gift from me. There is one last treasure I have left to give away. All these years I've saved it just for you." And from his rickety, rundown wagon the king brought out his throne.

"It's really quite comfortable," the king said. "And just the thing for long days of sewing."

From that day on the king often came to the quiltmaker's house in the clouds.

By day the quiltmaker sewed the beautiful quilts she would not sell, and at night the king took them down to the town. There he searched out the poor and downhearted, never happier than when he was giving something away.

Visit the quiltmaker and the king online at
**www.QuiltmakersGift.com**
where you will find:

 Puzzles and games from
*The Quiltmaker's Gift.*

 Stories of generosity from
around the globe.

 Quilt block lore and quilting
activities for all ages.

 Contests and prizes.

 Conversations with the
author and artist.

Jeff Brumbeau, Gail de Marcken, and
Scholastic Inc. have joined in dedicating
a portion of the revenue from
*The Quiltmaker's Gift* to projects that implement
the spirit of generosity portrayed by
the quiltmaker and the king.